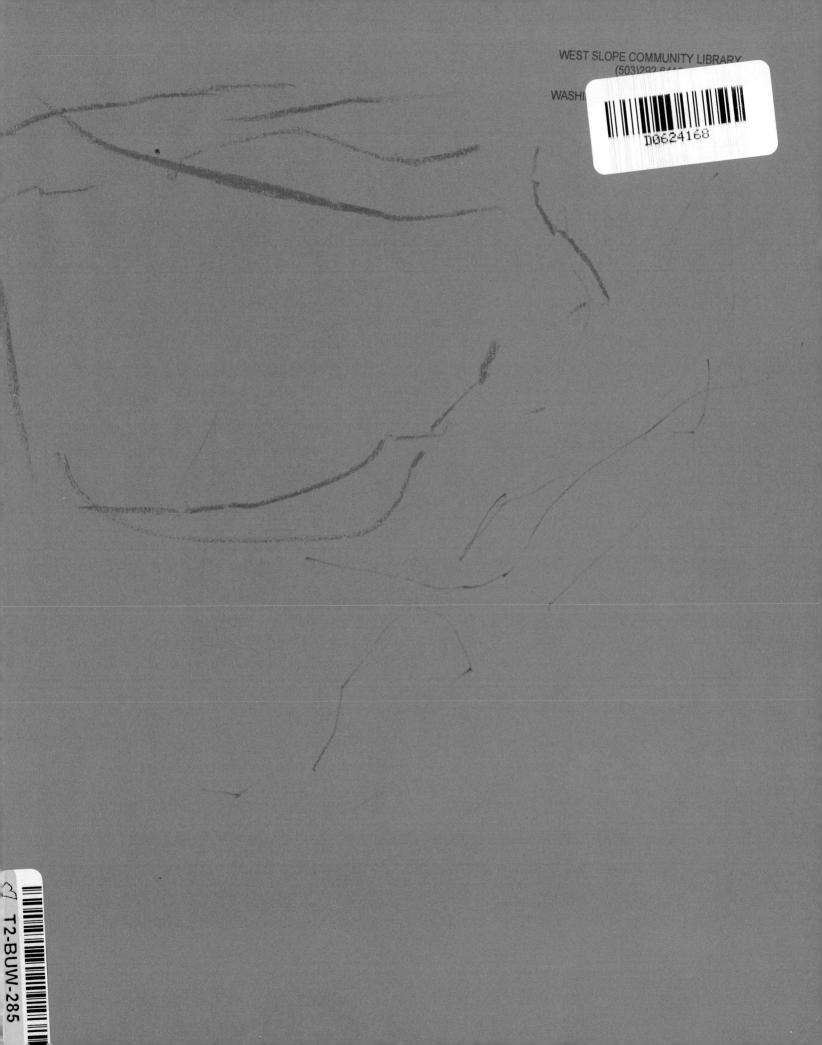

PORKENSTEIN

by KATHRYN LASKY

illustrated by DAVID JARVIS

THE BLUE SKY PRESS • AN IMPRINT OF SCHOLASTIC INC. • NEW YORK

To Max and Meribah, who gave me the idea
(and with apologies to Mary Shelley)
—K. L.
To Janina, my wife
—D. J.

THE BLUE SKY PRESS

Text copyright © 2002
by Kathryn Lasky
Illustrations copyright
© 2002 by David Jarvis
For information regarding
permission, please write to:
Permissions Department,
Scholastic Inc., 557 Broadway,
New York, New York 10012.
SCHOLASTIC, THE BLUE SKY PRESS,
and associated logos are
trademarks and/or
registered trademarks
of Scholastic Inc.
Library of Congress
catalog card number:
00-067997
ISBN 0-590-62380-x
10 9 8 7 6 5 4 3 2 1
02 03 04 05 06
Printed in Singapore   46
First printing, September 2002
Designed by Kathleen Westray

D r. Smart Pig was a famous inventor, but he didn't have any friends. His two brothers had been eaten by the Big Bad Wolf a year ago, and he had been very lonely ever since.

"Tomorrow is Halloween," he thought sadly. "What fun is Halloween without any friends?"

Suddenly he had an idea. "I'm an inventor. I can invent a friend! I'll never be lonely again!"

Dr. Pig was excited. He ran to his laboratory.

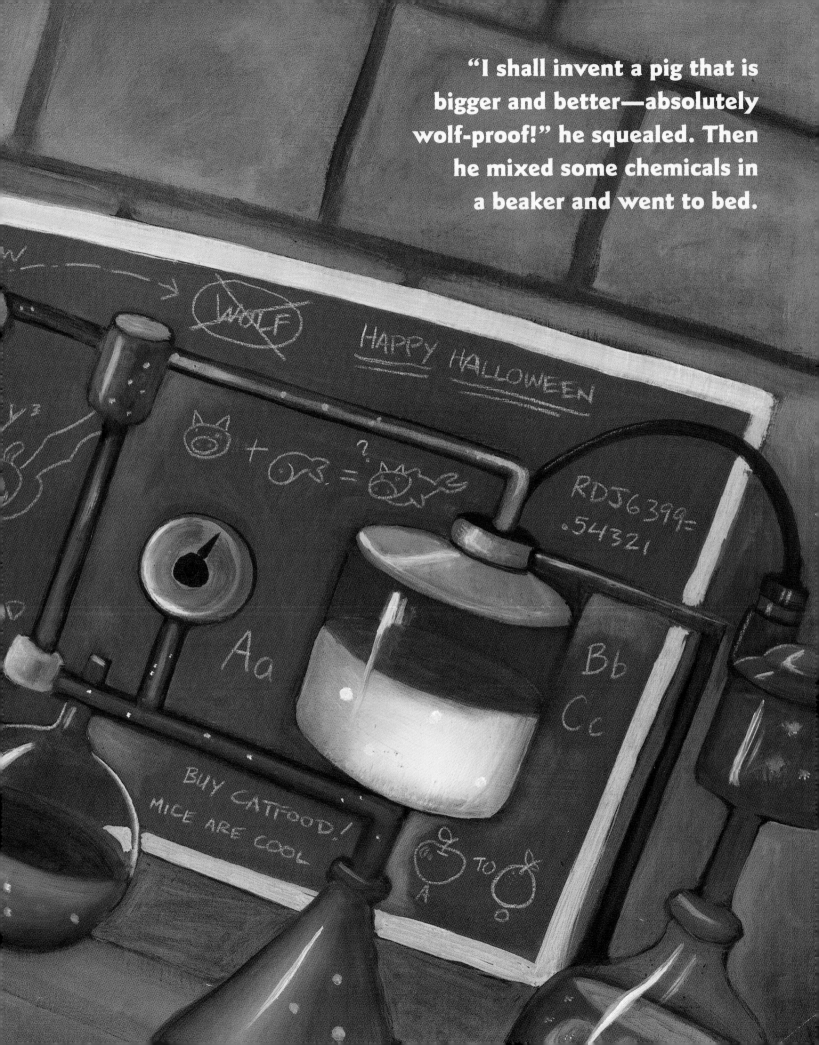

"I shall invent a pig that is bigger and better—absolutely wolf-proof!" he squealed. Then he mixed some chemicals in a beaker and went to bed.

At dawn, Dr. Pig raced to his laboratory. The beaker glowed mysteriously. Then something leaped up and squirted him in the eye.
"Oh, dear," cried Dr. Pig. "Something's gone wrong! I've invented a pig fish!"

He put the pig fish into an
aquarium and began to mix up a
new batch of chemicals, this time
with less salt. He put the beaker
into an incubator to keep it warm,
and off he went to weed his garden.

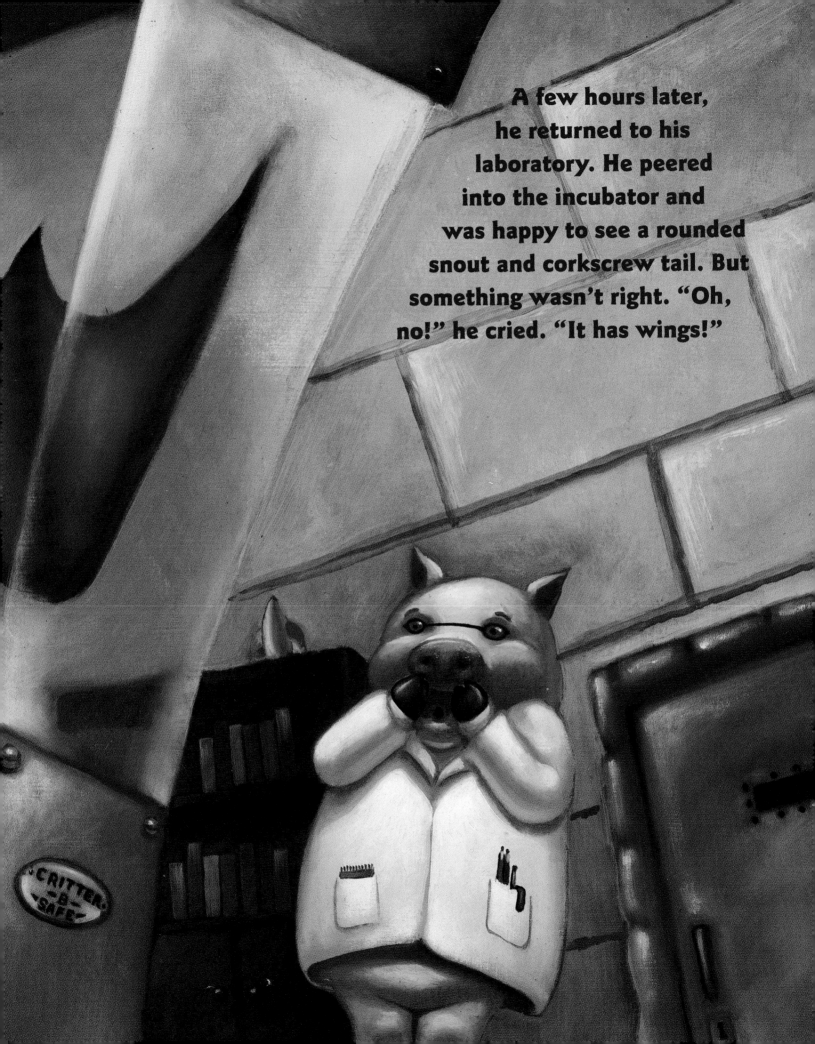

A few hours later, he returned to his laboratory. He peered into the incubator and was happy to see a rounded snout and corkscrew tail. But something wasn't right. "Oh, no!" he cried. "It has wings!"

The creature oinked, flew
off, and hung upside down
from the ceiling.
"It's a pig bat!" Dr. Pig said.
"I'll have to try again."
Halloween night was getting
closer, and Dr. Pig still did not
have a friend. He mixed up
another batch of chemicals, and
this time he hooked the beaker
up to his Electro-Pig-o-Meter.
At the last minute, he threw
in a teaspoon of sugar.

It was almost sunset when he heard loud grunts
coming from the lab. Another creation had come to life.
There, on the table, was the biggest pig he had ever seen.

"I'm starving!" the giant pig
shouted. "I need food. FEED ME!"
Dr. Pig gasped. "Would you like
a jelly doughnut?" he asked.
The giant pig swallowed it in one
gulp, dribbling jelly all over himself.

"MORE!" he shouted.
"FEED ME MORE!"
Dr. Smart Pig was worried.
Maybe inventing a friend
wasn't such a good
idea after all.

The new pig ate and ate and ate.
He ate jars of jam and peanut butter
and every bit of food in the house.
Then he ate the garbage,
including the can.

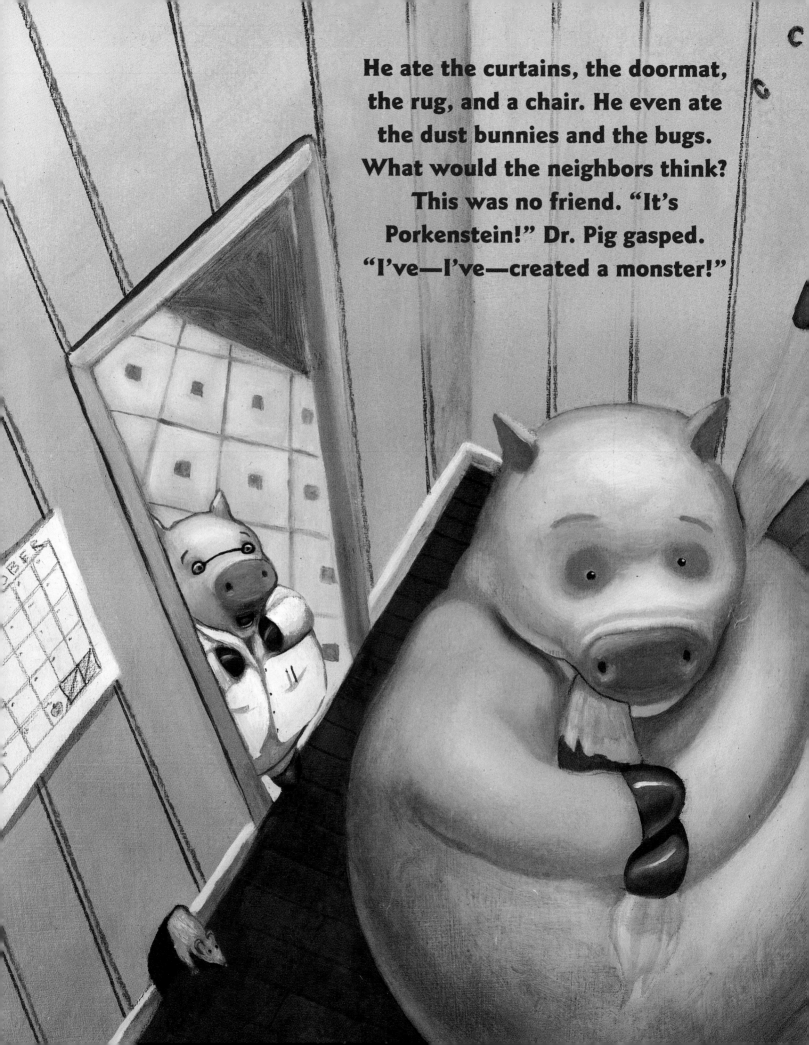

He ate the curtains, the doormat, the rug, and a chair. He even ate the dust bunnies and the bugs. What would the neighbors think? This was no friend. "It's Porkenstein!" Dr. Pig gasped. "I've—I've—created a monster!"

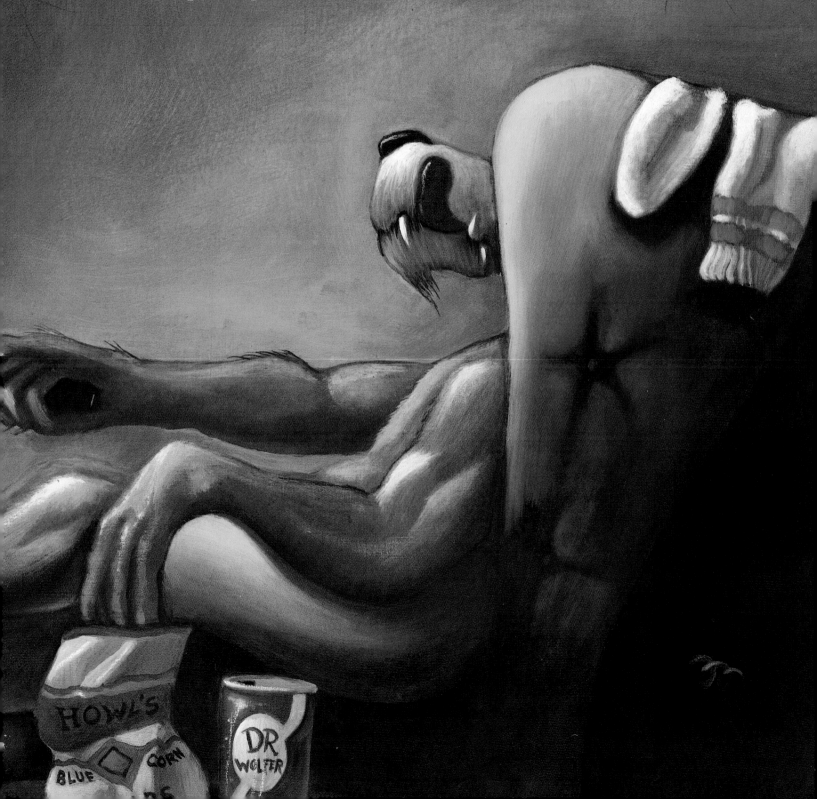

It did not take long for stories about Porkenstein
to spread. Soon everyone for miles around
was talking about the enormous pig.
The Big Bad Wolf heard about the incredible hog,
and he began to drool at the thought.
"Yum, yum, yum," he said to himself. "What a meal!"

It was just after sunset on Halloween night when someone knocked on Dr. Pig's door.

"Oh, no! Our first trick-or-treater, and you've eaten all the candy!" Dr. Pig began to cry.

Outside was a drooling little old lady with fangs, long furry ears, and a tail tucked up under her dress.

"It's *him!*" Dr. Smart Pig whispered,
and he began to shake with fear.
"Who?"
"The Big Bad Wolf, the one who
ate my brothers!"

Porkenstein opened the door.
"Trick or treat, piggie pie," the wolf said
in a creaky, old-lady voice. He licked
his chops. "You sure are a big fellow.
What big thighs you have."
"And what long furry ears
you have!" replied Porkenstein.
Inside the house, Dr. Pig listened, frozen
with fear. Suddenly there was a scuffling
sound—followed by a huge gulp and
a rumbling belch. Then silence.

Dr. Smart Pig peeked out the door.
"You didn't!" he said and gasped in disbelief.
"I did." Porkenstein smiled. A pair of
empty boots stood where the wolf had been.

That night, Dr. Pig could not believe how lucky he was. "Porkenstein," he said, "I'll never have a better friend."

"You mean I'm not just
an invention?" Porkenstein asked.
"No, you're a true friend."
The Big Bad Wolf was gone forever,
and Dr. Pig would never
be lonely again.

Now it was time for fun.
"I'm still HUNGRY!" said Porkenstein.
"Let's go trick-or-treating!"
So the two pigs put on costumes,
and off they went.